The
purple
Snerd

PA

The Purple Snerd

Rozanne Lanczak Williams
Illustrated by Mary GrandPré

Green Light Readers
Harcourt, Inc.
San Diego   New York   London

www.harcourt.com

First Green Light Readers edition 2000
Green Light Readers is a registered trademark of Harcourt, Inc.

Library of Congress Cataloging-in-Publication Data
Williams, Rozanne Lanczak.
The purple snerd/Rozanne Lanczak Williams; illustrated by Mary GrandPré.
—1st Green Light Readers ed.
p. cm.
"Green Light Readers."
Summary: When an imaginary creature appears under the porch, Fern looks
in her book to determine its name, decides it's a purple snerd, and spends
the day playing with it.
[1. Imaginary playmates—Fiction. 2. Stories in rhyme.]
I. GrandPré, Mary, ill. II. Title.
PZ8.3.W67926Pu 2000
[E]—dc21 99-50810
ISBN 0-15-202654-1
ISBN 0-15-202661-4 (pb)

A C E G H F D B
A C E G H F D B (pb)

One morning in March,
Fern was sitting outside.
Then all of a sudden . . .
"Snort! Chirp!" something cried.

It was under the porch.
Who or what could it be?
Some long purple fur
was all Fern could see.

It was smaller than her horse.
It was bigger than a bird.
Fern couldn't believe it—
could this be a Snerd?

The first thing Fern did
was to open her book.
Then she sat on a step
and had a good look.

Purple Snerds, the book said,
will purr, bark, and chirp.
When they eat all their sweet snacks,
they will snort and slurp.

Curled under Fern's porch,
the thing chirped, barked, and purred.
It snorted and slurped
like a Purple Snerd!

It said, "Hello, Fern!
I'm so glad we've met!
Can you find some sweet snacks—
as sweet as they get?"

"You *are* a Snerd!" cried Fern.
"Big and purple, I see!
I saw Snerds in my book
and now one's here with me!"

Fern and the Snerd
played around and had fun.
They even played Snerdball
outside in the sun.

Their time went by fast,
and the Snerd had to go.
"So long, Fern," he chirped.
"I'll come back, you know."

"So long," called Fern.
"It was such a fun day.
Bring more Purple Snerds
to my house to play!"

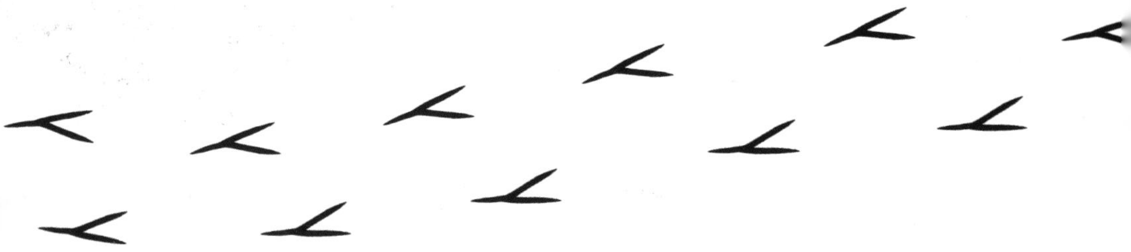

Meet the Illustrator

Mary GrandPré kept thinking of her dog, Charlie, when she tried to draw the Purple Snerd. Charlie has a hairy face and loves to eat sweets. Somehow, the Purple Snerd turned out to look a lot like Charlie! Besides drawing, Mary likes to visit schools. She tells children about her work and shows them how to draw, too.

Mike Woodside